THIS
BOOK
BELONGS

TO _____

Disney's
SMALL WORLD LIBRARY
PET PALS
An Adventure in Peru

GROLIER ENTERPRISES INC.
DANBURY, CONNECTICUT

Mickey, Minnie, and Pluto were upon a mountaintop high in Peru. They were visiting the ruins of Machu Picchu, the fortress city that was once part of the ancient Incan Empire.

Mickey glanced down at his guidebook. "It says that the Incan people lived here more than five hundred years ago. They were known for building great cities and roads. And this," he said as he walked over to a circle of giant stones, "was the Temple of the Sun."

"No wonder," said Minnie. "From up here it seems like the sun is close enough to touch!"

Just then Pluto tugged hard at his leash—so hard he pulled it out of Mickey's hand!

"Wait! Pluto!" Mickey called.

But Pluto was off and running after a shaggy animal that looked like a cross between a sheep and a camel.

"He's chasing that animal!" Minnie exclaimed.

"Pluto, come back here!" Mickey shouted.

Pluto did not obey Mickey. Instead, he ran past a big stone pillar called the Hitching Post of the Sun.

Mickey and Minnie wanted to get a better look at the giant sundial, but Pluto was running so fast they didn't have time to stop.

"I can't catch my breath!" Minnie gasped, stopping to rest.

"Neither can I!" agreed Mickey. "The air way up in the mountains doesn't have as much oxygen as the air down below. Since you and I aren't used to mountain air, it's hard for us to breathe."

"There's Pluto!" Minnie interrupted. "He's heading down the terraces!" She pointed to a series of wide, grass-covered steps leading down the steep mountain. Incan farmers had built the terraces to hold the crops in place so they wouldn't slide down the mountain during heavy rainstorms.

Mickey and Minnie ran down the terraced mountain after Pluto. They finally stopped by the banks of a stream. Mickey and Minnie looked all around, but there was no sign of Pluto. Then they saw a little girl filling a basket with what looked like mud.

"Have you seen our dog?" Mickey asked.

The girl nodded and smiled. "He went that way," she said, pointing. "Would you like me to help you find him?"

Mickey and Minnie introduced themselves to the girl, whose name was Juanita. They thanked her for offering to help.

The three started walking along the stream.

"Look!" Juanita cried, pointing to some paw prints in the mud. "He must have gone this way."

"Pluto can't be far away!" Mickey said.

The three new friends followed Pluto's tracks to a clearing where they saw a pair of the strange-looking animals. Pluto was peeking out cautiously from behind a bush.

Mickey and Minnie chuckled when they saw the nervous dog. Mickey walked over to Pluto and gently patted his head.

"You silly dog!" Mickey said. "These llamas don't look very dangerous."

"They aren't dangerous at all," Juanita said, "but they aren't llamas. They're called vicuñas. Vicuñas are smaller than llamas, and their wool is softer."

Minnie reached her hand toward one of the vicuñas. The animal's long hair felt very silky.

"Long ago, wool from vicuñas was used to make the robes for all the Incan leaders," Juanita explained. "Now it makes the best Peruvian blankets, coats, and sweaters."

"Thank you for helping us find Pluto," Mickcy told
Juanita. "He's always getting into trouble, but I love him
anyway!"

Juanita smiled. "It must be wonderful to have a pet.
After I sell my beads at the market tomorrow, I'm going to
buy a pet, too! Have you ever seen a cavy?" she asked.

Mickey and Minnie shook their heads.

"A cavy is a guinea pig," Juanita explained. "They're
really cute. And tomorrow I'm going to buy one for my
very own!"

"But first you must make your beads," a friendly voice called.

"Mama!" Juanita said.

Mickey and Minnie turned to see a pretty woman wearing a colorful hat. Juanita introduced her new friends to her mother.

"I'm pleased to meet you," Juanita's mother said to Mickey and Minnie. "I came to tell Juanita to come home for dinner."

"But I don't have enough clay to make my beads," Juanita said worriedly.

"We can help you," offered Minnie. "After all, you helped us find Pluto."

Soon they were all gathering clay. After the basket was filled, Juanita's mother invited Mickey and Minnie to dinner.

"And if you'd like, I can show you how I make the beads," Juanita said.

"I'd love to learn," said Minnie.

"Me, too," said Mickey. "And now that you mention dinner—I'm starving!"

On the way to Juanita's house, they met her brother, Pedro, who was bringing the family's flock of llamas home after a day of grazing.

"How do you like taking care of llamas?" asked Mickey.

Pedro tossed a soccer ball high in the air, then bounced it skillfully off one ankle and then the other. "The llamas aren't much trouble," he said. "And practicing soccer keeps me busy."

With a happy bark, Pluto joined Pedro in the ball game.

Pedro put the llamas in their pen as the sun dipped behind the mountaintops and the air became cold. They were all glad to step inside the snug adobe house where Juanita's mother had dinner cooking.

In a few minutes, they were seated around the table with Juanita's father.

"This is quinoa," Juanita's mother said, giving Minnie a generous helping of tiny, cooked yellow seeds.

"It tastes wonderful!" said Minnie after she took a bite.

Mickey tasted the bean soup. "This is delicious, too," he declared.

Juanita's father beamed with pride. "We grow these beans, as well as potatoes and barley on our farm," he told the guests. "Most of the families who live around here are also farmers."

After dinner, Mickey and Minnie helped Juanita roll the damp clay into a thin, flat slab.

"It's almost like making cookies," Minnie observed.

Once the clay was flat, they formed it into a long tube. Then they cut the tube into short sections the size of beads, and Juanita's mother baked them.

After the beads were baked and cool enough to touch, they were ready to be painted. Juanita showed Mickey and Minnie how to paint the bold, geometric designs the Incas used on their pottery.

"This is fun!" Mickey said.

"These beads really are beautiful," Minnie told Juanita. "I think a lot of people will want to buy them at the market."

While the beads were drying, Mickey and Minnie listened as Juanita's father played traditional Incan music on a panpipe.

Minnie watched in fascination as Juanita's mother twirled a special stick to spin llama wool into yarn.

"Would you like to learn?" she asked Minnie.

"Sure!" Minnie agreed.

    While Minnie learned how to spin yarn, Pedro gave
Mickey a knitting lesson. He explained that many boys in
Peru like to knit.
    "I sell these sweaters at the market," said Pedro.
"That's how I earned the money for my soccer ball."

Pluto watched the yarn bob up and down. Suddenly he seized the yarn and ran around the room, tangling himself up before Mickey could stop him. Everyone laughed as they watched Mickey chase the silly dog.

"Pluto can't help getting into trouble," Mickey said, smiling as he gave Pluto a big hug.

"Having a pet is a good way to make new friends," Mickey added.

"You're right," said Juanita. "I can't wait to have my own pet!" she added excitedly.

As soon as the paint on the beads was dry, Juanita showed them how to string the beads into pretty necklaces.

After all the beads were strung, Mickey and Minnie thanked their new friends for a wonderful time and arranged to meet them at their house the next morning.

The following day, Mickey, Minnie, and Pluto went with Juanita and her family to the city of Cuzco, which once had been the capital of the Incan Empire. At the marketplace, they strolled past booths full of beautiful crafts. There were brightly striped hats and belts, handknit sweaters, and pottery.

By the time they reached Juanita, there were
only a few strands of beads left. Juanita beamed at
Mickey and Minnie.

"Thanks to your help, I made so many necklaces that
I have enough money to buy *two* cavies!" she said
happily. "Will you help me pick them out?"

The three friends headed over to the booth where cavies were sold. There were so many cute cavies, it was hard to decide which ones to choose. Juanita finally settled on two fluffy brown ones.

"I'm going to name them Mickey and Minnie," she announced, "to remember your visit to Peru."

As Mickey and Minnie laughed, Pluto gave an approving bark.

Did You Know...?

There are many different customs and places that make each country special. Do you remember some of the things below from the story?

The Incas were an ancient Indian people who lived in Peru and created one of the richest empires in the early Americas. The Incas were great builders, warriors, and artists.

Machu Picchu (MAH-choo PEEK-choo) was the "secret city" of the Incas. This walled fortress was built on a high ridge between two mountain peaks to protect the Incan empire.

Nearly half of Peru's people are Indian. There are more Indians here than in any other country in the Americas.

The vicuña (vih-KOON-yuh) lives high in the Andes mountains of Peru. Like its cousin the llama, the vicuña is a member of the camel family. It is said to have the finest, softest wool of any animal.

The Andean Indians love to eat quinoa (kah-know-ah), a special grain grown nowhere else in the world. These Indians also grow more than 300 different kinds of potatoes, including a purple one!

Cuzco (KOO-sko) was once the capital city of the Incan empire. It had palaces and temples decorated with gold. Today the city has many beautiful churches. It is a center where farmers sell their crops and merchants their woolens and pottery.

Panpipes, a musical instrument made up of small wooden pipes, are played on fiesta days in Peru, along with drums, flutes, and small harps. People dress in colorful costumes and masks, and dance to the lively music.

The Indian craftspeople of Peru create a dazzling variety of beautiful beads, pottery, jewelry, and handwoven blankets.

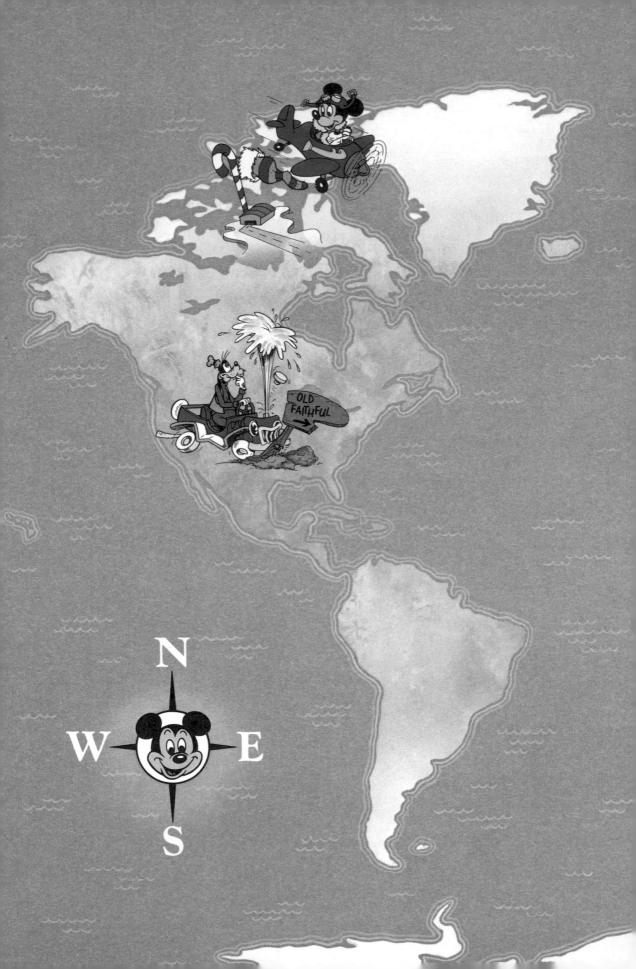